Ransom Neutron Stars
Deep in the Dark Woods
by Cath Jones
Illustrated by Kate Morgan

Published by Ransom Publishing Ltd.
Unit 7, Brocklands Farm, West Meon, Hampshire GU32 1JN, UK
www.ransom.co.uk

ISBN   978 178591 426 3
First published in 2017

Deep in the Dark Woods

Cath Jones

Illustrated by Kate Morgan

Ransom

Can you see Nam and Lin and her big, fat dog, Bong?

Nam and Lin are deep in a dark wood.

Nam took Lin for a fantastic picnic, but he forgot to load the picnic bag in the van!

Now it is dark, but the moon is high and Nam has a torch.

Has Nam got the right gear?

Yes. He has a wigwam for the picnic.

He paid for a good wigwam in the shop.

He got lots of bits of kit and a big bed!

They need food and Nam has no picnic.

The wood has a deep river.

Nam gets into his boat and looks for fish in the deep part of the river.

He hangs bait on a hook and waits.

Can Nam get a fish?
Will he fall in?

Bong the dog looks at Nam and wags his tail.

Lin needs wood to cook
a fantastic supper.

She chops up an oak.

Then she digs up carrots
and a radish.

Now she sits down and waits
for Nam and his fish.

Look! Nam did not fall in and he has a fish!

Quick, get herbs!

Lin picks and chops herbs to go with the fish.

She puts the fish, carrots, radish and herbs in tinfoil.

Now they wait for the food to cook.

Is supper fantastic?

No! But it is not bad.

Bong has a carrot for his supper.

Now Lin and Nam need a coffee!

Will Nam and Lin and her big, fat dog Bong fit in the wigwam?

Nam and Lin let Bong join them in the wigwam.

Yes, they all fit in. It is a big wigwam!

Lin and Bong curl up.

Nam sighs. The big dog fills the bed. Not much room for him!

Now Nam sits in the porch
with his torch and a book.

He can see rain, but he is not
wet.

Not yet!

Now Nam sees lightning.
The rain turns to hail and
falls hard on the wigwam.

The wigwam is torn
and soon rain soaks in.

Was Nam mad to get Lin in a wigwam in winter?

If Lin gets wet, will she moan?

Will Bong bark and yap?

Look! The wigwam falls down.

Oops! The rain is too much.

It is such a shock for Lin. She quits.

"Nam, let's go!"

With a sigh, Nam, Lin and Bong the big, fat dog go back to the van.

They will be back
in the summer.

They will be back with a
bigger, better wigwam
for a fantastic picnic!

Bong wags his tail.

He cannot wait!

Have you read?

Ben's
Jerk Chicken Van

by Cath Jones

Night Combat

by Stephen Rickard

Have you read?

G B H

by Jill Atkins

Steel Pan Traffic Jam

by Cath Jones

Ransom Neutron Stars

Deep in the Dark Woods
Word count **429**

Covers:
Letters and Sounds Phase 3

Phonics

Phonics 1	Not Pop, Not Rock Go to the Laptop Man Gus and the Tin of Ham	*Phonics 2*	**Deep in the Dark Woods** Night Combat Ben's Jerk Chicken Van
Phonics 3	GBH Steel Pan Traffic Jam Platform 7	*Phonics 4*	The Rock Show Gaps in the Brain New Kinds of Energy

Book bands

Pink	Curry! Free Runners My Toys	*Red*	Shopping with Zombies Into the Scanner Planting My Garden
Yellow	Fit for Love The Lottery Ticket In the Stars	*Blue*	Awesome ATAs Wolves The Giant Jigsaw
Green	Fly, May FLY! How to Start Your Own Crazy Cult The Care Home	*Orange*	Text Me The Last Soldier Best Friends